*This book is dedicated to
Katja and Sascha, two amazing
and creative sisters.*

Read all the adventures in the
Our Generation® Book Series

Read more about **Our Generation®** books and dolls online:
www.ogdolls.com

our
generation®

This is Dedra ana
Denelle's story.

DEDRA AND DENELLE™

THE VACATION OF HIDDEN CHARMS

BY

ERIKA NADINE WHITE

ILLUSTRATED BY GÉRALDINE CHARETTE

An Our Generation® *book*

MAISON BATTAT INC. *Publisher*

CONTENTS

EXTRA! EXTRA! READ ALL ABOUT IT!
Big words, wacky words, powerful words, funny words...
what do they all mean? They are marked with this symbol *.
Look them up in the Glossary at the end of this book.

Chapter One

I SPY, YOU SEA

One Friday night in the spring, Dad arrived home from work carrying a huge package and set it down on the kitchen table. My sister, Denelle, and I immediately deserted the bowl of carrots we were scrubbing at the sink and ran over to see what it was. Mom adjusted the heat under a saucepan full of stew and wiped her hands on a dish towel. She had a big grin on her face as Dad kissed her hello.

"You got it?" she asked him.

"I got it," he answered. We had no idea what our parents were talking about, but we were really curious, as we tore open the package and saw what was inside.

"Flippers?" I looked up at Dad.

"You and Denelle will need them, Dedra, for swimming in the ocean!" Dad answered.

The ocean! Wow!

Dad explained that he had finally been able to arrange for some time off work. My sister and I jumped for joy. We hadn't had a family vacation since Dad and his partners opened their first outdoor sports store five years ago, so we were very excited.

We had been to the ocean before, but not in a long time. In our living room, there is a picture of me and Denelle, sitting on a picnic blanket on a beach. We're about two and a half years old. My sister and I don't really remember that vacation, but my parents told us that we would be going back to the very same beach. This time we'd be old enough to remember every minute!

After that first night, Dad brought home "vacation equipment" regularly—beach towels one week, butterfly nets the next—until it seemed we had everything we could possibly need for our trip.

‧‧‧ ‧‧

Finally the big day arrived. We got up super early to help Mom and Dad pack the car. Mom had made lists of everything we needed to bring. Our suitcases were packed with sandals, swimsuits, and sundresses. Dad fastened his new kayak to the roof rack and strapped our boogie boards* tightly beside it.

Denelle brought board games, cards and paper dolls, as well as a big box of markers, crayons and colored pencils. Her book bag was overflowing. She also insisted we needed all of our rain gear in case we had "a nice rainy day." Denelle loves rainy weather, but I was hoping for sun, sun, sun! I packed our butterfly nets, our new snorkels and flippers, and a ton of beach toys. Mom added an activity kit for each of us, full of fun things to do on the drive.

Last of all, I stuffed all of our favorite pillows and blankets into the back seat so we could have a cozy journey.

When we were done, Dad looked in the car and said, "There's not enough room back here for you two!"

"Yes there is!" we answered as one. We do that a lot. Denelle and I are twins. Not identical, but fraternal. That means we don't look alike, and sometimes we don't act alike, either. All the same, we've always been best friends as well as sisters. We even wear matching necklaces with pendants that fit together like a puzzle. When you put the two pendants together it makes a whole heart. Grandma gave them to us when we were really little. She told us, "These charms were made to go together, just like you two!" We hardly ever go anywhere without them.

Dad reorganized the back seat to make a bit more room. Mom looked at all her lists and checked the trunk one more time. Dad asked, "Girls, have you got everything? Are you ready?"

Denelle and I looked at our jam-packed car, and then at each other. I touched one finger to her half of the heart pendant and she reached out and touched mine. We grinned at each other. We were pretty sure we hadn't forgotten anything important, but as long as we had our twin charms we were ready for anything.

"Let's go!" we cried, leaping into the back seat.

It was such a long drive! At first we sang songs, but after an hour or so Mom said that was "probably enough singing for now." She thought it might be a good time for doing something quiet. Denelle took out her book and started to read. I sorted through my activity kit, which had stickers and puzzles and games, but I was having a hard time sitting still. For a while I tried doing a crossword puzzle but it felt a bit like homework.

"What's a five letter word for nice weather?" I asked.

"You can figure it out, Dedra!" answered Dad.

Mom murmured "Hmm?" She was looking at a map.

"Rainy!" answered Denelle. I knew that wasn't right, because the word started with "S." Using block letters, I filled the squares in: S I L L Y. Then I put the crossword away.

Finally, it was time to stop for lunch and stretch our legs. We had a picnic by the side of the road at a little rest stop*. That was nice, but we were back on the road in no time because we wanted to get to the ocean before dark.

I stared out the window for ages. We had left all the towns and suburbs behind us and a deep forest was all I could see on either side of the road. *This drive is driving me crazy!* I thought. I tried to rearrange my pillows so I could sleep, but I couldn't sleep. While I was trying to get comfortable, my activity bag flipped over and the stickers fell out everywhere, so I had to pick them all up.

I guess I was driving Denelle a bit crazy, too, with all of my fidgeting, because finally, with a small sigh, she put her book away and asked me if I wanted to play "I Spy." We were really in the country now. We spotted fields, farms, tractors, two hawks, cows, some sheep and a lot of cars. After a while we started spotting marshy areas and seagulls.

Finally Denelle cried, "I spy with my little eye something big and blue."

I groaned, because we always use that clue when we can't think of anything better, but this time it wasn't the sky, which was starting to turn sunset pink. Suddenly I saw the ocean, showing just beyond the next curve in the road.

"Hurray! We're nearly there!" we both cried.

Chapter Two

A DAY AT THE BEACH

We pulled into the parking lot next to a row of beach cottages. Shadows were stretching across the sand. The ocean seemed to go on forever. While our parents picked up the keys, and then carried all our stuff into the cottage, Dedra and I ran around, exploring everything.

The little cottages were so cute! They stood in a long row beside the water. Bicycles and beach toys were lined up next to some of them.

"Look!" said Dedra, "There must be tons of kids here!" I nodded, but I wasn't really all that curious about meeting other children. I had been looking forward to a quiet holiday, just us and our parents, hanging out in our cottage, reading books (I brought a huge pile), and playing board games.

In the little yard behind our cottage was a

picnic table and a huge hammock strung between two trees. In front there was a fire pit on the beach, practically right outside our door. Dedra was pretty excited about that, but I thought our room was the best!

It was in a little loft above the kitchen. You had to climb a sort of stepladder to get up there and, once you were up, you could slide it along a railing to make more room downstairs. We'd never seen a sliding ladder before, and we'd certainly never slept in our own loft. I couldn't wait to settle in and get all of our things organized.

We rolled out our sleeping bags and piled up our pillows. I found a shelf for my books. While we got set up in the loft, Mom made tacos. We went to bed right after supper because it was already so late.

❧ ❦

When I woke up in the morning, I was alone in the loft. My sister had gotten up before me. I stretched lazily, and then read the last chapter of my book. I could smell good things happening

in the kitchen so I went downstairs to help Mom make pancakes. Dad and Dedra came in while we were cooking. They'd already gone for a hike.

"Guess what, Denelle!" said my sister. "There are trails all through the woods where you can hike or ride a bike! And there's a salt marsh* not far away, and an ecomuseum*!" I was pretty excited to hear that. I love learning about different animals and their habitats*.

"I got some great maps," said Dad, spreading them out on the table and showing us the places my sister had mentioned, not far from where they had been hiking.

"Next time I want to come, too!" I told them.

"Me, too," said Mom, as we all sat down to stacks of hot pancakes. It was a perfect vacation breakfast!

After we'd eaten, Dedra wanted to go to the beach right away, but first we had to do the dishes. By the time we climbed up to the loft to get into our swimsuits, she practically had ants in her pants*. She threw her suit on quickly, and then scampered down the stairs to go and get her boogie board. I put a beach cover-up over my suit, and began sorting out a few things to bring along. Finally, I was ready to go. I climbed down from the loft with my full bag slung over my shoulder.

Dedra was already standing by the door, hopping on one foot as Mom said, "Towels? Sun hats? Sunscreen?" She looked us over and held her hand out. "Better give me your necklaces, too. You don't want to lose them in the ocean."

"What?" I cried. "Why? We won't lose them, we promise!" but my sister was already unfastening the clasp on her chain.

Dedra shook her head at me. "Mom's right. We'd feel awful if we lost them. Besides, I want to surf some waves!"

So I took off my necklace, too, and dropped it into Mom's hand.

It felt weird, but Dedra caught my eye. "It's OK," she whispered. I wanted to believe her, so I tried to smile. I knew she understood how I was

21

feeling. We hardly ever take our necklaces off. At the same time I could tell that Dedra wasn't as bothered by it as I was. She was too busy thinking about swimming.

So was Dad. He slung a towel over his shoulder, clapped his hands, and said, "Look out, ocean! Here we come!" Mom grabbed the beach bag, and we all trooped out the front door onto the hot, sandy beach.

By the time we settled on a spot to set up our beach chairs, blankets and sand toys, I had decided that the waves looked awfully big. It was a beautiful, breezy day, but I didn't really feel like swimming.

"Go ahead with Dad," I told Dedra, "I want to work on my paper dolls." Mom said that was fine, since she needed to relax for a while after that big breakfast. Besides, she had a book she wanted to read.

"Suit yourself," Dedra told me, "but Dad and I are going to master these boogie boards way faster than you if you don't come in and practice!"

I didn't even answer. I was busy getting out my markers and scissors. Dedra was already halfway to the water.

"Enjoy the beach!" Dad smiled at Mom and me as he grabbed a boogie board and followed my sister into the waves.

Chapter Three

A WHALE OF A TIME

Dad and I had fun playing in the surf and falling off our boogie boards while Mom and Denelle sat on a blanket under a big beach umbrella. By the time we stopped for a picnic lunch, I was exhausted. After a cucumber sandwich and some apple juice, I was happy to sit quietly for a while, playing with all the new outfits Denelle had cut out and colored in while I was swimming. Her paper dolls are always very well dressed and stylish because she's really good at coming up with great colors and combinations.

After that, we collected some shells and washed them off in the ocean. We brought them over to the blanket to show Mom and Dad.

"They're really pretty," said Mom, "but we can't keep them."

"Why not?" asked Denelle.

"Well, because they're part of the local ecosystem*. That means they belong here."

I guess we looked disappointed, because Mom continued, "Don't worry, we can take photos of them, or draw pictures, or find another way to remember all the treasures we're going to discover on our vacation."

"Like what other way?" asked Denelle, but I didn't hear the answer, because just then I noticed a bunch of kids and families had arrived and were setting up nearby. They seemed to be sorting out all kinds of equipment. I was still staring when two of the girls ran over to where we were sitting.

"Hi," said a redheaded girl with long pigtails, "I'm Kelly Ann, and this is Jodie." Jodie waved a flipper at us and grinned.

"Hi!" Denelle and I said.

"Are you staying in the cottages?" asked Kelly Ann.

"Yes," we answered.

"So are we!" said Jodie. "Want to snorkel

with us? My parents are going to give us a lesson, and we have some extra equipment.

"Oh, I'd love to, but we have our own equipment right here!" I cried, pulling our brand new snorkels and flippers from the beach bag.

"Maybe I'll just stay here," began Denelle, but Mom interrupted.

"Oh, Denelle, you've been sitting here with me for hours. It's a perfect opportunity!"

Dad nodded, "The conditions couldn't be better!" The wind had died down while we were having lunch and the waves were much smaller. The sun was getting awfully hot and the water looked cool and inviting, at least to me. Denelle made a face but grabbed a snorkel and her flippers.

Mom and Dad walked with us a little way down the beach, where we met two other girls who were waiting with snorkeling equipment of their own. One was named Suyin. Her friend was Vienna. Vienna and her baby brother were staying in the cottage right beside ours. While we were talking to the girls, our parents started laughing and hugging Suyin's mom and dad.

"The Chans! What a coincidence!" cried Mom. She explained that Suyin and her family had also been on vacation here the last time we visited, when we were practically babies. So we'd met Suyin before, but we didn't remember it. Neither did she, but our parents sure were glad to see each other again.

After everyone calmed down, Mom and Dad introduced themselves to Jodie's parents, who turned out to be actual certified scuba diving instructors*. I could tell Denelle was relieved that we would be snorkeling in shallow water, not diving to the bottom of the ocean with oxygen tanks, but I thought I would love to try scuba diving some day, when I'm older. In the meantime, Jodie's parents gave all of us a lesson in how to snorkel properly.

First, before we even got into the water, we had to adjust our masks.

"Hold the mask to your face and breathe in. Now take your hand away. Did the mask stay on?

28

Good! You've got the right fit! Remember, if air can get in, water can, too!" Jodie's mom helped us adjust the straps so the masks were comfortable.

Next, we waded into the water to get our feet wet and slip on our flippers. They felt funny, like big frog feet, and we all had a good time splashing around in them.

"Now, your snorkel has to be comfortable and sit at the right angle," called Jodie's dad above the noise of our frog splashes. We strapped the snorkels in place and the grownups checked to make sure we'd done it properly. First we tried breathing through the snorkel with our heads above water, just to get used to the nozzle. Everyone looked so funny wearing masks and snorkels, like creatures from the watery deep, but as soon as we stopped giggling long enough to take a few breaths, the snorkels worked just fine.

Finally, we gave it a try underwater. Sometimes, if you put your head to the side, or a big wave splashes you, water can get inside the breathing tube, so Jodie's dad showed us how to get water out of the snorkel by blowing hard into the nozzle. We all practiced together. I pretended I was a whale, spouting*. I imagined we looked like a family of little whales in brightly colored swimsuits.

Then Jodie's parents showed us how to float on our bellies, using the flippers to move without spending too much energy on swimming. It was pretty easy! I floated along, barely flicking my flippers, looking through the mask. I saw some tiny fish with pretty silvery flecks on their tails.

Suddenly there was a big commotion and a whole lot of splashing. I stood up in a hurry and pulled off my mask. Jodie's dad was hauling my sister out of the water. Denelle was crying and coughing at the same time. Mom and Dad came running to see what was wrong.

Chapter Four

SOMETHING'S FISHY*

I hate the ocean, I hate snorkeling, and I *especially* hate fish! At least, that's how I felt at the time. I'd never been so scared in my life!

First of all, it was hard enough trying to breathe through the snorkel, look through the mask, and float all at the same time. I was also trying to avoid getting splashed by Dedra and the others, because I really didn't want any salty seawater getting in my snorkel.

Just as I was finally getting the hang of it, an enormous shark swam right up into my face! OK, it wasn't a shark, and it wasn't that big, but it was a pretty big fish. At least I thought it was a fish. It might have been somebody's flipper.

Anyway, I screamed and the tube fell out of my mouth. Then water got in, and it felt like I was

drowning. I don't know why I didn't just stand up, because the water wasn't over my head, but I guess I was too frightened to think. If Jodie's dad hadn't been there to pull me out, who knows what could have happened. I was coughing and it felt like I had swallowed about half the ocean.

Mom and Dad hugged me until I stopped crying. My sister patted my shoulder. The lifeguard looked me over and said I was fine. I didn't feel fine, though. I certainly wasn't going to get back in the water, even though Dedra and the other kids wanted me to. When I felt a little bit better, Mom took me back to the cottage while my sister stayed on the beach. Dad stayed, too. It seemed like they didn't even care that I nearly drowned!

꙳ ꙳

When Dad and Dedra came back to the cottage for dinner, the first thing Dad said was, "Feeling better, Denelle?" but as soon as I answered, "Yeah, I guess," he quickly changed the subject. Soon everyone was talking nonstop about everything except my terrifying accident.

Dad was excited because he had discovered that Suyin's and Kelly Ann's families also brought kayaks. He kept talking about how much fun it was to take a break and spend time with different people. Then Dedra went on and on about what a great swimmer Jodic is, and how fun it was learning to snorkel, until I thought I couldn't stand to listen to one more word.

After dinner, Dedra wanted to go out and play horseshoes with all the other kids. She wanted me to come, too, but I didn't feel up to it. My tummy was still upset from the seawater. I just wanted to go to bed early with a good book. I read for a long time, but I could hear my sister and the other kids playing on the beach, and it was sort of hard to focus on the story. I was so tired, but I couldn't fall asleep until my sister finally came in and got ready for bed, too. As soon as she climbed up to the loft and whispered "Sweet dreams," I felt my eyes starting to close.

The next morning I was hoping we could all do something together, but Dad wanted to go kayaking with Mr. Chan and Kelly Ann's big brothers, and Dedra wanted to go to the beach with Jodie and her family. I decided to just hang around the cottage. Mom had claimed the hammock. She was reading a book. I draped towels over the top of the picnic table to make a fort, and stretched out on a beach mat underneath, where it was nice and shady, with my coloring books and some comics. We spent a quiet morning. *I'm perfectly happy here*, I thought. *Who needs to swim?*

ᴥ ᴥ

When Dedra came home for lunch she found me still under the picnic table. "Are you coming to the beach this afternoon?" she asked, lifting the edge of a towel and squatting down to look at me. "We're going to have a sandcastle contest and a swimming race!"

Yuck and yuck, I thought. Sand in my

35

swimsuit, water up my nose. I shook my head and she rolled her eyes at me.

"Come on Denelle, you're missing all the fun!"

"I'm having plenty of fun," I insisted, even though I was getting maybe a little bored with being alone in my picnic table fort.

"Fine," she said, dropping the towel in my face and running into the cottage where Mom was making some sandwiches. I climbed out from under the picnic table and followed her inside.

"Mom," I called, "may I have my necklace? I'm not going to swim today, anyway."

"Sure," she answered, grabbing her purse. "It's right here." She slipped her hand into the little zippered pocket where she always keeps our special things. Her face fell. "Oh, they're not in here!" she said in surprise.

"What!" Dedra and I exclaimed. "What do you mean? Where could they be?"

This was a disaster*! We searched high and low but couldn't find them anywhere. Mom said she must have put them somewhere safe. Dedra looked in the sugar bowl. They weren't there. I examined every inch of the kitchen floor on my hands and knees but they weren't there either. Mom dumped her whole purse out on the table, and we sifted* through the contents, but no necklaces.

By this time I was crying. Dedra was pretty upset, too, but she just kept saying, "They can't be far. Necklaces don't just disappear!" I knew she was right, but by the time we sat down to eat, I could barely even swallow my sandwich.

After lunch, Jodie and her mom knocked on the door to see if we were coming back to the beach. Mom said to go ahead, but I shook my head, and Dedra left without me.

Chapter Five

HIDDEN CHARMS

I was so worried about the necklaces and my sister that I couldn't enjoy the beach. It was frustrating*. I just wanted to relax and have a good time, but I kept wondering where the necklaces could be. Denelle seemed really upset, and it wasn't just our missing charms. Ever since the snorkeling accident, she didn't even want to come near the water!

Vienna and Suyin were building sandcastles right by the edge of the water when we arrived, so Jodie and I started on our own, with tall towers and courtyards* paved with shells. We built a big moat* around all of the castles, which looked really neat until the high tide* started flooding the walls. We declared every one of our castles a prizewinner, and Jodie's mom took pictures of us

posing with our creations before they disappeared. Then the ocean lapped at the towers like they were ice cream cones and by the end of the afternoon our castles were just lumps of sand.

We went snorkeling again with Jodie's parents, but the whole time we were in the water I kept thinking about Denelle's accident with the "shark" and how scared she had been. Maybe if she just gave snorkeling one more try she'd find out how easy it is. She'd even see that the fish were small, and kind of pretty, not big and scary like she thought.

I just couldn't stop thinking about everything that had happened, and how Denelle must be feeling. Finally I decided to go back to the cottage, but when I arrived only Mom was there. Dad and Denelle had gone into town to pick up some pizzas.

While we waited for them to come back, I hunted for the necklaces. Mom said I could go through her purse again, so I sat down at the kitchen table and took out every single item in case they were wrapped around a hairbrush or hiding in a packet of tissues, but they weren't.

Next I checked to see if they might have slipped through a tear in the lining of the purse. There was a tiny rip in one corner, and we found some change and a few bobby pins, but no necklaces. Mom got out a needle and thread to fix the rip, and while she sewed tiny stitches, she told me she was sure they would turn up.

"Like you said yourself, Dedra, the necklaces didn't get up and walk away. I just can't think where I could have put them. As soon as we stop worrying about it, we'll find them."

By the time Denelle and Dad got back to the cottage, we were all so hungry that I kind of forgot about the whole problem for a while. We had delicious pepperoni pizza, with brownies for dessert, and played board games until it was bedtime.

My sister and I were both so sleepy when we climbed into the loft that we never ended up talking about the necklaces, or why Denelle didn't want to come swimming. We just turned out the light, said goodnight, and crawled into bed. Denelle didn't even read her book!

The next morning we were all up early. Mom and Dad were sitting at the kitchen table having coffee when Denelle and I came down from the loft. I looked out the kitchen window and saw Kelly Ann's brothers setting up a volleyball net on the beach. Jodie and Vienna were tossing a ball back and forth.

"Let's go get in on the game!" I cried. My sister was already pulling eggs and bacon out of the fridge.

"Forget that!" I told her, grabbing a box from the pantry. "Let's have cereal, it's faster!"

"I'm not in a rush," Denelle answered. "Don't you want to relax? We're on vacation! I want to eat with Mom and Dad!"

"No, I don't want to relax! I want to go out

and play, not be a stick-in-the-mud*!"

"OK, girls, don't argue," said Dad, as he reached for the frying pan. "If Dedra wants to have cereal, that's fine. The rest of us will have eggs." He looked straight at me, wearing his serious face. "Denelle can join you when she's ready. Agreed?"

"Yes, Dad," we both answered. I was already finishing my bowl of cereal and flying out the door.

Volleyball is one of my all-time favorite sports, and absolutely nothing beats volleyball on the beach!

It wasn't like a real game, we didn't keep score, but that didn't matter at all. I could have played all day. We ran into the water to get the ball when the wind stole it from us, or chased it down the beach, stumbling in the warm sand.

It wasn't just a kids' game, either. Kelly Ann's brothers were really good. So were Jodie's parents and Vienna's mom. People kept coming and going, taking breaks to swim or snack or surf.

I looked for my sister, but there was no sign of her all morning.

Denelle never did join the volleyball game. I found her reading in the hammock out back when I came back to the cottage for lunch.

"How come you never came to the beach?" I asked when I saw her.

Denelle looked up from her book. "I don't know," she said. "I just didn't feel like it."

Just then Mom brought some sandwiches out to the picnic table and called us over. We sat down to eat. "Dad and I are having lunch in the kitchen," she told us, adding, "Don't forget to bring your plates in when you're done."

"We won't!" we promised.

We ate our sandwiches in silence for a few minutes. It seemed as if Denelle was mad about something, but I wasn't sure what.

"Well, are you going to come swimming after lunch?" I asked, finally. "Everyone's meeting back at the beach in half an hour."

"You go ahead," Denelle answered. "I think I'll just hang out here."

"You can't! You're missing everything!" I insisted. "How often can you swim in the ocean?"

Denelle frowned. "Let the fish swim in the ocean. They can have it!"

"Fine, suit yourself!" I said, and stomped into the kitchen with my empty plate.

Chapter Six

OCEANS OF TROUBLE

I sat alone at the picnic table, with my half-finished sandwich in front of me. I knew Dedra wanted me to come swimming, but I was mad at the ocean. If it weren't for the ocean, we never would have had to take our necklaces off in the first place. Plus, I would never have had that horrible snorkeling accident! *Anyway,* I thought, *we should be trying to find those necklaces, not fooling around on the beach.*

Dedra came back out of the cottage with her towel slung over her shoulder and grabbed her boogie board from the rack beside the door. She stared at me sitting glumly* at the picnic table and looked sad herself.

"Look, I'm sorry I stomped off," she began, "I just really wish you would come to the beach and have some fun!"

"How can I? How can *you*? Our necklaces are missing! Don't you even want to look for them?"

"I have been!" Dedra exclaimed. "Mom and I looked for ages yesterday while you were in town with Dad. We turned her whole purse inside out!"

"You did? Well, I didn't know!" I cried, my eyes filling with tears. "You don't even tell me what's going on anymore!" I blinked furiously.

"Because we're never together for me to tell you! You don't want to do anything but stay by yourself, reading books and coloring!" Dedra was practically yelling.

"That's not true! You're so mean." I shook my head in disbelief.

"I'm not mean, you're the one who doesn't want to have any fun!" Dedra paused for a second and took a deep breath. "Look, this is silly. Let's just stop fighting. I'm going to the beach. All the kids are there. When you're ready to stop feeling sorry for yourself you can come and join us!"

"Don't talk to me like that. You're not Mom," I hissed.

"Well, you're acting like a baby!" said Dedra. I couldn't believe my ears. Just then Dad came out the back door.

"You two aren't arguing again, are you? Come on, girls, you know better!" He turned to me. "Denelle, don't you want to come to the beach?"

"Maybe after," I answered, looking down. "I want to help Mom tidy up first."

"OK," he said, "we'll see you later. Don't just hang around the cottage all day!"

"OK, Dad," I answered.

The tears I'd been trying to hold back started leaking out as soon as they left. I felt so dumb. I didn't know Dedra had been looking for the necklaces yesterday. I hadn't even thought of searching for them myself. So why was I so mad that Dedra didn't want to look for them right now? It felt as if we were having one disagreement after another. It seemed like the only way to fix it would be to find our necklaces!

I looked down at the remains of my sandwich, which were kind of soggy now, and brought the plate into the kitchen. Mom saw me crying and gave me a big hug.

"What's wrong?" she wanted to know.

"Me and Dedra haven't stopped arguing since we lost the necklaces! Now I'm afraid we'll never get along again!"

"Don't worry," Mom told me, "I know you and Dedra love those necklaces because they show how you feel about each other. But it's not the charms that make you two so special, they're just a symbol*!" She smiled. "Love isn't like jewelry—it never gets lost, and you can always find it if you try." Mom stroked my head. "You know what? We can always replace the necklaces, but it's your relationship with your sister that is one of a kind!

I wiped my eyes. Mom was right. With or without the necklaces, I just had to find a way to stop arguing with Dedra.

We tidied up the kitchen, and then Mom said we should get out of the house. I really didn't want to swim. I just felt nervous about that big, wavy ocean full of big, weird creatures.

"Can't we do something else, Mom? There's no way I'm getting on a boogie board or snorkeling again! Dad and Dedra hardly ever get out of the water! They won't mind if we don't join them!"

"Well," said Mom, "there is the ecomuseum. Do you want to hike over and check it out?"

Did I? You bet! We went down to the beach to see if Dad and Dedra wanted to join us, but sure enough, they were boogie boarding with a whole bunch of people. From the edge of the sand, using a combination of yelling and hand signals, we made it clear that we'd meet back at the cottage later on.

∽ ∾

The ecomuseum was amazing. It was on a salt marsh, with raised wooden platforms where you could walk around outside, see birds, and read information panels about salt marshes and how they help keep the environment healthy. Inside was also a small aquarium, and rooms set up for all the different parts of the local habitat.

A really nice guide named Carrie showed us around and answered all our questions. She was a marine biologist*. I told Carrie about the shark I thought I saw when I was snorkeling, and she didn't laugh or anything. She was really interested.

"It does sound like a false alarm," she told me, "but you weren't wrong to wonder, because there are lots of sharks in the ocean. Blue sharks, dogfish, basking sharks..."

"Wow, really?" I'd thought I was being silly worrying about them.

"Yep, at least thirteen different species are here in the summer!"

"Only in the summer?" I asked.

"Some sharks are travelers. They visit when the weather gets warm." Carrie smiled, "Just like some people!"

Sharks come in all shapes and sizes, which I hadn't realized. Carrie showed us a bunch of illustrated charts. "This type of shark is called a dogfish. They're pretty common around here. Fishermen don't like them, because they eat so many fish, but they're harmless to people."

It wasn't very scary. I was way bigger than it. Carrie pointed out a huge one, saying, "We also have basking sharks, the second largest fish in the ocean. This guy doesn't have any teeth—he eats plankton*." I was much bigger than plankton!

We looked at pictures of other sharks, and Carrie even let me hold an actual shark jaw with rows of tiny, sharp teeth.

"This shark jaw comes from a blue shark. They like deep, cool water," Carrie explained.

"So, would any shark ever come on the beach?" I had to ask, just to be sure. I thought Carrie would say no, but I was surprised.

"Well, it happens," she replied. "A great white might, by accident. They like to eat seals, so sometimes they come quite close to shore when they're hunting." I made a mental note to keep my distance from seals.

"Great whites are protected," Carrie continued, "which means people are not allowed to harm them. In fact, our researchers fly around in planes, keeping an eye on them! Some sharks are even tagged* so that we can track their movements!"

Carrie explained that knowing where sharks are helps us to understand more about them, so we can protect them. It's also a good way of making sure they don't get too close to swimmers!

"Don't worry," she assured us, "the lifeguards are not just keeping an eye on you; they see everything in the water! They would know right away if a shark were nearby. If one does come close to a beach, we put up a purple flag. That means to stay out of the water!"

After visiting the aquarium I knew that what I had seen was definitely a flipper, not any sort of fish. Actually, sharks are really interesting animals. Now that I knew more about them they didn't seem as scary.

We wandered through models of tidal flats and forests. These habitats have to be protected, because they are fragile. That's why you can only bike or hike on the trails. All kinds of animals live near the ocean, and some of them are endangered, like the piping plover, which is a really pretty little bird. To protect animals, we need to protect the land and the water, too.

Now I understand about leaving shells where they belong, because the sand is actually partly made up of tiny shells crushed by the tide. Without shells, there wouldn't be a beach!

Chapter Seven

FRIENDSHIP AFLOAT

When Dad and I got down to the beach with our boogie boards, lots of our friends were already there. Suyin's dad waved my father over to a blanket where he was sitting with Jodie's family, and they all started talking about kayaks.

Jodie and Vienna ran over to me. Vienna called out, "Hey, can we see your boogie board?" I held it out so they could have a look, but when Jodie saw my face, she asked, "What's wrong?"

"Nothing," I answered, heading down to the ocean and floating my boogie board in the shallow water. I sat down on it and it sank into the soft sand where the beach met the sea. The cool water splashed my legs and tummy. Vienna and Jodie sat down beside me. I didn't know how to say what I was feeling.

Suyin swam over to us. "Where's Denelle?" she wanted to know.

"Helping my mom tidy up," I answered, glumly.

"Is she coming to the beach?" Suyin persisted.

"I don't know." I sighed. "Denelle doesn't really like swimming in the ocean."

"Because she got scared snorkeling the other day?" asked Jodie.

"I guess," I said, but I thought it was more than that somehow. "She's really upset, too. I mean, we both are, because we can't find our necklaces."

"What necklaces?" asked Vienna.

"Our twin charms. They're really special. Mom said we had to take them off to go swimming, and after that we couldn't find them. We've been looking everywhere!" I felt like I wasn't explaining very well, but Suyin seemed to understand.

"Poor Denelle! It's like she thinks the ocean makes bad things happen!" she exclaimed.

"Exactly!" I answered, "and the worst part

is that I bugged her to come swimming so much we ended up having a big fight!"

"Don't worry, it'll be all right!" said Jodie, smiling.

"What do you mean it will be all right?" I cried, "Denelle is super mad at me!"

"Well," Jodie explained, "It's too bad she's mad at you, but Mom always says that arguments happen when you really need to talk about how you're feeling. Maybe you two just need to talk."

It sounded kind of crazy to me, but I knew that Jodie and the other girls were trying to make me feel better, and maybe in a way she was right. If Denelle and I could stop arguing, we'd both be having more fun.

എ എ

Dad came down to the water then, carrying his boogie board. Kelly Ann and her family had arrived, and they had boogie boards, too. We all took turns riding the boards and horsing around* in the waves.

Eventually, Mom and Denelle did show up on the beach, but they were dressed for hiking and didn't come down to the water. They called to us something about visiting the ecomuseum, but I was having a great time right where I was. I couldn't imagine getting out of the ocean to go hiking in the hot sun.

Dad didn't want to go either, so we just waved and yelled that we'd catch up later on. As they turned and walked away, my stomach flip-flopped, and I thought about running after them, but just then Dad lifted me onto a boogie board and I felt like I was flying.

Later, though, when we took a break, I started worrying again. I lay on my towel, sipping some apple juice, staring out at the ocean while Jodie and Vienna talked about a movie they had both seen. Maybe I should have gone to the ecomuseum with Mom and Denelle. It seemed like I'd hardly seen my sister in the last two days.

"I used to be scared of the ocean," said Suyin, out of the blue*. It was like she knew what I was thinking.

"Really? You seem to like it now!" I was surprised.

"We've been coming to this beach for years and years, but I wouldn't go in the water until last summer."

"How come?" I wondered.

"I don't know." Suyin shrugged*. "I guess it just seemed so big and, you know, splashy. But then I took lots of swimming lessons back home, and once I got to be a really good swimmer, the ocean didn't seem as scary."

"Hmm. Denelle is already a pretty good swimmer, because we've had lots of lessons, too."

"I'm still sort of afraid of the ocean," confessed Vienna. "I would never swim without my mom!"

"Or my parents," said Jodie. "You like swimming with them, right?"

"That's true," Vienna said. "Maybe you just

need to let Denelle know we'll all keep an eye on her and make sure she's OK."

"Maybe," I said. I frowned. In order to really solve this problem, I knew I had to talk to Denelle.

"I wonder if she's back from the ecomuseum yet? Maybe I should go check in at the cottage."

Just then, Jodie's mom came over. "Guess what!" she announced, "Tonight we're all going to have a big feast* together. Dedra, I just called your mom. She's going to get some bread at the bakery. Do you want to come to the fish market?"

"You bet!" I said. "Yippee!"

Chapter Eight

FULL MOON FEAST

As we were leaving the ecomuseum, Mom got a call on her cell phone. All the beach families were planning to have dinner together. Finally, a group activity that didn't involve swimming!

Mom and I walked along the trail to the edge of the village, and at the bakery we filled two shopping bags with fresh baked rolls and big loaves of crusty French bread.

We went slowly on our way back to our cottage, carrying the fragrant* bags of bread. Mom and I talked a bit, pointing out pretty wildflowers that grew beside the trail, but mostly we were quiet, enjoying the view.

I was still thinking about everything we'd seen at the ecomuseum. As we climbed a little hill, the ocean came into view. The sun was setting and birds were soaring in a pink sky over lavender water. It was beautiful, like a painting, but even better because it was real life. I could see that the ocean was a very pretty part of the picture.

"Having a good time?" asked Mom.

"Yes," I smiled at her. "I'm having a great time."

Back at the beach, Kelly Ann's brothers were building a bonfire in the pit. Jodie, Kelly Ann and Dedra were swinging in the huge hammock behind our cottage. Suyin was lugging a huge sack of corn on the cob out to the picnic table.

"Want to help me shuck some corn?" she asked.

"Sure!" I answered. I love shucking corn— the way you peel the husks back to reveal the golden kernels, and the corn silk sticks to everything, so you have to pick the threads off one by one. Suyin said it was one of her favorite chores, too. She's really nice. We started talking about books and found out that we have almost exactly the same tastes! In fact I had brought book number four of a series we both loved, and Suyin was only up to book three, so I said I would lend her my copy.

Every family contributed something different. We had so much food! All the kids sat on a big blanket together and had a picnic. I tasted a bit of everything, but the lobster was my favorite. Fresh, sweet and dripping with garlic butter!

"I don't know how you can eat that!" said Vienna, munching a veggie dog. She wouldn't touch the lobster. I know lots of kids who don't like seafood, but Dedra and I have always had what Dad calls "adventurous appetites."

"I love lobster," I said, "almost as much as vacations!"

"Me, too!" said Dedra. "Vacations are best, but lobster is next!"

We all laughed and I smiled at my sister. It felt like we were getting along again.

We had ice cream for dessert: chocolate or vanilla. I chose vanilla. So did Dedra.

It was a warm night, with just a bit of a breeze. We all sat around talking until the sky was dark and full of stars. Jodie and Kelly Ann told us about a million knock-knock jokes. Jodie would say "Knock-knock!" and before she was even finished speaking, Kelly Ann would answer, "Who's there?"

"Who!"

"Who who?

"Just came to see if you're *owl* right!"

We laughed until we were all holding our bellies.

After dinner we gathered around the fire. The moon rose over the water. It was full, and made a bright road of light across the ocean. Kelly Ann's dad brought out his guitar and began to play.

"Hurray!" cried Dedra and I, clapping our hands. We love a sing-along*! Everyone started calling out the names of their favorite songs.

"Hold on!" Kelly Ann's dad said, "Let me take one request at a time!"

Starting out with campfire favorites, we made our way around the circle, everyone choosing a song they wanted to sing. We did "The Green Grass Grew All Around," "Down by the Riverside," "Little Green Frog" and lots more. I knew the words to some of the music, but some I had never heard before, so it was fun to learn new lyrics*.

When we were all too tired to sing anymore, we made s'mores*. Dedra and I roasted the marshmallows over the fire, Suyin placed the chocolates on the crackers, and Jodie and Kelly Ann squashed the gooey treats together and passed them out to everyone. By the time we went to bed, my sister and I were so stuffed we could barely climb the ladder to our loft.

Chapter Nine

SURPRISE SHOWERS

The next morning we all slept in. When I sat up, Denelle was just opening her eyes. Still wearing our pajamas, we climbed down from the loft.

"Mom!" cried Denelle, "Can we do something all together this morning?"

"That's the plan!" said Mom, scooping two apples out of the fruit bowl and handing one to each of us. "Have an apple. Make some toast or cereal. After breakfast we're all going to hike to the salt marsh."

"You'll love it!" Denelle told me. She was right. It was beautiful, full of birds and bright sunlight flickering through tall grasses.

By the time we got back to the cottage for lunch, it was getting really hot.

"Do you want to come to the beach after we

eat?" I asked Denelle. I didn't say anything about swimming, hoping that would encourage her, but I was expecting her to make another excuse. She surprised me.

"Sure," she said, "That was quite a hike! I could use a little splash to cool off!"

"Really?" I beamed* at her. "I'm so happy you're coming!" I really was happy, but I wondered what had happened to make her change her mind.

❧ ☙

We got our swimsuits on in a jiffy* and ran out of the cottage and onto the beach. It was so nice having the ocean right at our front door! Mom and Dad set up beach chairs and Denelle and I sat at the very edge of the water, with the waves rolling in over our legs.

"Are you still mad at the ocean?" I asked.

Denelle smiled. "No," she said, "I was at first, but really I think I was more scared than angry."

"Because you blamed the ocean for bad

things happening? Like losing our necklaces?"

"How did you know?" Denelle stared at me. "I was embarrassed about the snorkeling thing, too. Everyone must have thought I was being a real scaredy-cat*!"

"No, I don't think so. Suyin told me she didn't like swimming in the ocean until last year, and Vienna still won't go in without her mom."

"Well, I'll go in with you!" announced Denelle, jumping up and splashing into the waves. I followed her happily and we drifted along the shoreline together, not really swimming, kind of crawling with our hands in the sand and our bodies floating in the water.

"So what made you change your mind about swimming?" I had to ask.

"I don't know. I like swimming—you know that. It took me a while to get used to the ocean, but I think I've decided I like it after all." Denelle grinned. "Besides, if I don't get in the water, I'll never see you!"

I smiled back at her, but I suddenly

remembered the argument we'd had yesterday, and I felt terrible.

"You know, yesterday, after lunch? I'm sorry I called you a baby." I said.

"That's OK," Denelle laughed, "but I was being a scaredy-cat, not a baby!"

We'd drifted down the beach as far as the lifeguard's chair. There weren't many people on the beach today. A family with two little toddlers was down at one end, and a group of older people was having lunch, but we didn't see anyone we knew.

"I'm happy you changed your mind," I told Denelle.

"I'm happy we're not arguing anymore!" she answered.

"Me, too," I said. Denelle never holds a grudge. I felt lucky to have such a nice sister. I reached over and gave her a wet, salty hug.

Denelle looked back up the beach to where our parents were sitting, near our cottage.

"Race you back to home base*!" she challenged me.

"You're on!"

It was hard to swim very fast because the waves keep pushing us sideways, and we were giggling as the ocean rolled us around and pulled us away from our goal. In the end it was a tie, which it often is when it comes to me and my sister.

ᦔ ᦔ

Soon Mom and Dad joined us in the water and we all tried the boogie boards together. Mom was terrible, but Dad was starting to get pretty good. Denelle hadn't done it before, so she was just getting the hang of it when I noticed the sky filling up with dark, angry clouds. Thunder cracked and I saw a streak of lightning in the sky.

The lifeguard blew her whistle and ordered us all out of the water. We picked up our gear and ran for the cottage, but the rain was too fast for us.

"So much for swimming!" I cried as we burst through the door. "Now what are we supposed to do?"

Mom grabbed a pile of clean, dry towels and

wrapped them around our soaking wet, shivering shoulders.

"First thing, let's get tidied up!" said Mom. A little puddle of sand and water was pooling around our feet. Dad handed me some paper towels and I stooped to wipe up the mess.

"Next, dry clothes!" he ordered.

It took a while, but finally we were clean and dry. Mom and Dad cooked supper while Denelle and I made a salad. We ate delicious blueberry crumble for dessert. It was so yummy!

We had a fun night with our parents, playing dominoes and board games. The rain kept spattering on the roof, but inside our cottage it was bright and cozy.

"Except for our missing charms, that was a perfect day!" Denelle told me, as we were getting ready for bed. I agreed with her. In spite of the rain, which I knew Denelle liked anyway, it had been a pretty nice day. Things were looking up; Denelle was enjoying the ocean, and best of all, we weren't fighting!

Chapter Ten

RAINY DAY SECRETS

We woke up to the sound of rain on the roof. It was a sound I loved, but Dedra looked miserable. She buried her face in the pillow and groaned, "Oh no! Not more rain! We'll be stuck inside all day!"

"Don't worry, Dedra. We brought our rain gear, remember?"

Dedra looked over at me, "But what will we do? It's raining too hard to swim or play on the beach!"

"We'll find something to do!" I jumped out of bed and pulled on a warm hoodie and some thick leggings. I tossed Dedra her favorite sweater and jeans. "Let's get some breakfast. I'm starving!"

"You're always starving!" teased Dedra, but she pulled her clothes on quickly and followed me down to the kitchen. Mom was fiddling with the radio and Dad was stirring up a big bowl of eggs.

"Looks like we're in for a whole lot of rain!" said Mom as the weather report ended. She tuned in to a classical station and the cottage filled with soft piano music. "Guess we'll have to find some indoor activities today."

"But Mom, we've got our rain gear!" I cried.

"That's true. I guess you can go out, as long as there's no thunder and lightning."

Dad scrambled the eggs and put a huge stack of toast on the table. We all dug in.

After breakfast, we helped wash the dishes and tidy up the cottage. When everything was shipshape* I asked, "Can we go visit the other kids and see what they're doing?"

"Sure," said Mom. "In fact I'll walk over with you."

I grabbed the book I'd promised to loan Suyin and stuck it in the inside pocket of my raincoat. Mom dug our rain boots out of the trunk of the car, and when we were all bundled up we dashed to the cottage right next to ours and knocked on the door. Vienna's mom opened the door. "Come on in!" she told us. "We've just been trying to figure out what to do with this rainy day!"

Vienna was looking sadly out the window at the rainy beach, but she brightened right up when she saw us. "Hey, you guys! What are you doing?"

"We're thinking of taking a walk in the rain," I told her. "Want to come with us?"

"Sure," she said. "Mom, where's my raincoat?"

We left our moms playing with Vienna's baby brother, promising to check back before we went any further than the end of our little row of cottages. At Kelly Ann's, we found not one friend, but two, because Jodie was already there. They were working on a huge jigsaw puzzle together but were happy to leave it and come out with us.

The five of us walked down the beach, the rain splashing patterns in the sand at our feet. The sky was gray, and so was the sea. The air was cool, but the rain was gentle.

At Suyin's, we were all invited in. When she saw us she jumped up from the table where she had been working, crying "What's up, you guys?"

"We're walking in the rain!" Vienna told Suyin. I gave her the book I'd promised to loan her.

"Ooh!" she said, "Hurray! Now I know what I'm reading at bedtime tonight!"

She ran to put it away and find her raincoat. While we waited, I looked around. The Chans' cottage was bigger than ours. Her mom is a professional artist and art supplies were everywhere. Suyin even had her own craft table set up by the window. On it were little sculptures and jars of bright paint. Suyin came back carrying her raincoat and rubber boots.

"What are you making?" I asked her.

"Oh, that's my hobby," said Suyin. "I like to make sculptures everywhere I go." I could see a little sandcastle, a lighthouse and a seagull.

"Wow! Those are amazing! You're really talented," I told her.

"We just made a fresh batch of play dough. Do you girls want to make some sculptures, too?" asked Suyin's mom.

"Not right now, Mom! We're going out to play in the rain," said Suyin. I was curious, though, so while everyone was getting ready to go back outside I asked Mrs. Chan a few questions. I had an idea, but I was going to need a bit of grown-up help.

Suyin found her rain gear and we all walked back up to Vienna's house together.

"What's that book you loaned Suyin?" Kelly Ann wanted to know.

"Oh, it's a great series!" I told her. "It's all about these six princesses who live on a very rainy planet, and in each book there's a different adventure..."

Suyin interrupted, "Like the one where the creatures from the desert planet try to steal all the water, and the princesses are the only ones who can stop them..."

"Six princesses in the rain?" cried Jodie.

"You've got to be kidding! That's just like us!"

"That's true!" I said. "There are six of us, too! Hey—we should play it as a game!"

So we did, up and down the beach, and in the backyards of our cottages, all afternoon. We had so much fun, all of the other girls said they wanted to read the series, too. I wrote down the titles so they would be able to find them at the library.

Later that day, some of the dads decided they would go into town to buy groceries and other supplies. When I heard about that, I ran to find Dad, and whispered in his ear about some special supplies that I needed. He smiled. I put my finger to my lips.

"Don't tell anyone yet," I made him promise.

Dad just winked and gave me his word*.

We played until we were so soaked, even in our rain gear, we all had to go home and change.

That night, just as we were getting ready for bed, Mrs. Chan called and asked to speak to me. We talked for a few minutes and then Mom got back on the phone.

"What's going on?" Dedra wanted to know, but I wouldn't explain.

"We have to collect more seashells in the morning," I told her.

"Why?" she wanted to know. "I thought we couldn't keep them anyway!"

"It's a surprise!" I grinned, "You'll have to wait and see!"

Chapter Eleven

SPE-SHELL MEMORIES

It rained for days, but with all of Denelle's great ideas for things to do I wasn't as upset about the weather as I might have been. The six rainy princesses were together constantly, and our parents were all hanging out together, too. We played at each others' cottages, created some very special memories, and went for long, wet walks on the trails and along the beach.

In between visiting and playing, Denelle and I kept hunting for our necklaces, but they just weren't anywhere in the cabin. Now that Denelle and I were getting along again, the missing hearts didn't seem to be as much of a catastrophe*, but we still wanted them back. Mom and Dad said they would get us new ones, but somehow that just wouldn't be the same.

Even though we couldn't find our own special charms, it turned out Denelle had a great idea for making new ones! I knew she had been planning a surprise, but it was really cool how she got Dad and Mrs. Chan to help out without any of us knowing about it.

Without explaining why, Denelle asked all of us to spend the morning hunting for the prettiest shells on the beach. Even though it was still raining, we had a great time stomping up and down in the sand and searching for treasure. When we were almost done, Denelle told us she had some things to do, and we should meet her over at Suyin's cottage in a little while.

When we got there, carrying pails of shells, a large table was set up near the window, covered in art supplies.

"Perfect timing!" cried Denelle. "Are you ready to make some memories to bring home?"

Fascinated, we all crowded around the table and Denelle unveiled her plan.

She and Mrs. Chan had figured out how to

make the most incredible plaster seashells.

First we made molds out of homemade play dough. We pressed our shells into the play dough to make a shell-shaped impression*. Then we poured plaster of Paris* into the molds. When we were done, we washed all the real seashells carefully and put them back on the beach.

Then we all went for a splashy, wet walk.

"I never would have imagined enjoying the rain this much," said Jodie, jumping in a puddle. "At first I thought, 'Oh no, my vacation is ruined!' But the last two days have been so much fun!"

"I know," I agreed. "At first I was mad, too, but we're all having such a great time!"

"Thanks to Denelle's great ideas!" said Suyin.

Denelle smiled. "It was you that gave me the shell idea, Suyin, when I saw your sculptures."

"Either way," Vienna broke in, "I'm having the best vacation ever! And at least we don't have to swim, right Denelle?"

"Actually," Denelle said, "I'm not afraid

of the ocean anymore. I was swimming with my family when the rain started."

"Really? What changed your mind?" Vienna wanted to know.

"I'm not sure...I guess going to the ecomuseum, learning about the ocean, and real sharks and what they're like, not just being scared of something I don't know much about."

"What do you mean, real sharks?" asked Kelly Ann.

"There are no sharks here, are there?" cried Vienna.

"Actually there are lots!" Denelle spent the rest of the walk telling us all about the different kinds of sharks in the water. At first Kelly Ann and Vienna looked terrified, but by the end they were smiling again. Jodie just kept nodding, because she knows a lot about ocean life from her parents.

Denelle explained how important sharks are to the ocean because they help keep it clean, which is important for every living creature. She told us how the researchers and lifeguards help keep us safe, and how to be safe ourselves, by knowing what to look for, and by following safety rules. By the time she was done we were all amazed.

"You sure learned a lot in one visit!" said Jodie.

"From now on, you're our ocean expert," Kelly Ann teased.

"From now on, I'll swim with Jodie's parents, my parents, or you, Denelle, because you must be paying pretty close attention!" exclaimed Vienna.

"Well," promised Denelle, "I will certainly tell you if I see a purple flag!"

We all laughed. It felt like we had all been friends forever.

                   ✿ ✿

The next day, when the plaster was hard, we carefully removed the play dough to find perfect replicas* of our shells. We spent a terrific afternoon decorating the plaster shells with paint, sparkles, and even some of Mom's nail polish, and let them dry in the breeze by the window.

When we were done, some of our shells looked just like the ones we'd been collecting on the beach. Others were very fanciful, and might have come from the rainy planet where six princesses were always having magical adventures.

That night after dinner, which was very crowded with so many families all packed into Suyin's cottage, we played board games and cards for ages. Later we played charades, and our team won easily because no one else could figure out the rainy princess book titles at all!

It was a wonderful day, and a really fun evening, but kind of sad, too, because Jodie's family was leaving the next day. Kelly Ann was leaving too, and we were going the morning after that, so this was going to be our last night all together. Suyin and Vienna were staying for the rest of the month. They were so lucky!

Before the evening ended the parents all exchanged phone numbers, e-mail and addresses, and we girls all exchanged special shells to

remember each other and our summer vacation together. I gave Jodie a pretty pink one. She gave me a green one with a picture of a little fish on one side.

I think the best one I made was a very special shell for my sister. I tried to make it look just like a real shell, with little orange stripes on the back, and I painted a heart inside it, sort of like our pendants. When I gave it to her, Denelle smiled and handed me one she'd been working on that was almost exactly the same!

Chapter Twelve

HAPPY HEARTS

I woke up to Dedra jumping up and down beside me crying, "Wake up, sleepyhead! It's time for some fun in the sun!" Sure enough, sunshine was streaming through the window in our loft.

Although I'd been enjoying our rainy holiday, I was happy it was nice weather for our last day at the ocean. Dedra and I got dressed quickly and bounded down the ladder for breakfast. We were in a hurry because we didn't want to miss the big send-off. All the families gathered by the cottages to say goodbye to our new friends. Standing with Suyin and Vienna, we waved goodbye to Kelly Ann and Jodie's families and wished them a safe journey home.

"I'll write to you!" Dedra called to Jodie as the car pulled away. They had decided to become pen pals*. Suyin and I were going to be pen pals, too.

We waved until the cars had disappeared in the distance, and then the Chans invited us to join them for a ride. Mr. Chan had rented a rowboat! I was a bit nervous at first, because the little boat really bounced around, but after I got used to it, I thought it was kind of fun. The boat had a glass bottom, and it was a great way to see fish without a snorkel! We spotted one pretty big one. Dad said it might have been a bluefish.

After our boat ride we had a nice picnic on the beach, with fried chicken and potato salad that Vienna's mom made while the rest of us were out on the boat. After lunch we started playing volleyball and swimming. We were in and out of the water all afternoon.

"I'm glad to see you got over your snorkel scare!" the lifeguard called to me, as Vienna and I ran by her chair on our way to join our families in the water.

"Me, too!" I told her. "It helps to know

you're keeping an eye out for us!"

"You bet I am!" she laughed, waving her binoculars at us. "Now go show me some serious swimming!"

Vienna and I raced into the water, splashing and laughing. Dad was doing a lazy crawl* up and down the beach.

I climbed on his back and yelled, "Give me a ride, you big shark!"

Dad rose out of the water with me on his shoulders. "Piggyback fight!*" he called.

Suyin jumped on her dad's back. "We challenge you!" she cried.

Vienna climbed up onto Dedra's shoulders. "Water princess power!" she cried.

You would think they had a disadvantage*, since Dedra is quite a bit shorter than Dad or Mr. Chan, but they were slippery, quick and hard to beat! We all wrestled in the water until we were laughing too hard to continue. It was a perfect afternoon.

My parents invited the Chans to our house

for supper, since we'd spent so much time in their cottage over the last few days. Vienna and her family came, too. Mom made a huge pot of spaghetti, and Dad made his special garlic bread. Mr. Chan liked the spaghetti sauce so much Mom gave him the recipe.

We've made some good friends here. Not just me and Dedra, but our parents, too. At the beginning of the vacation I wasn't sure I wanted to meet any new people, but now I'm really glad we all did.

After dinner, we said good night to everyone. I promised Suyin I would write to her as soon as we got home.

"We're going to miss you guys so much," Dedra told Vienna and Suyin.

"But we'll see you next summer, right?" asked Mrs. Chan.

"You sure will!" answered Dad. "From now on, this is our annual* vacation spot!"

"Yay!" We all clapped. I knew I was going to spend the rest of the year dreaming about our next vacation!

Mom and Dad cleaned up the cottage and we spent some time rounding up all our gear so we would be ready to leave first thing in the morning.

It was almost bedtime when Dedra and I came in from helping Dad load up the car.

Mom was sitting at the table, packing our freshly cleaned snorkels and fins into the empty beach bag. Suddenly she got a funny look on her face.

"Oh!" she laughed. "Not my purse, our beach bag!"

"What's that, hon?" asked Dad.

Mom held out her hand. "Look girls, here are your necklaces!" They'd been in the side pocket of the beach bag all along!

"Our charms!" squealed Dedra.

"Our hearts!" I cried. Mom quickly fastened them around our necks and we hugged each other, happy to have them again.

I'm so glad the necklaces aren't lost, but I'm even happier to know that they are a symbol, not a charm. It's a good thing we made up before we found them, just so I could be 100 percent sure!

The next morning we left really early, just as the sun was rising. No one else was up except the lifeguard.

"See you next year," we called. She waved to us.

See you next year, I thought, as I took a last look at the ocean and the beach cottages. I could barely wait.

"Ready, girls?" asked Dad. I touched one finger to Dedra's half of the heart pendant and she reached out and touched mine. We grinned at each other. With or without our special charms, we were two sisters who would always be ready for new adventures!

"Ready, Dad!" we cried as we jumped into the car.

Glossary

Many words have more than one meaning. Here are the definitions of words marked with this symbol * (an asterisk) as they are used in this story.

annual: *something that happens every year*

"ants in his/her pants": *not able to stand still; excited*

beamed: *smiled with excitement*

boogie board: *a small surfboard, ridden while lying down (also known as a bodyboard)*

catastrophe: *a terrible event*

courtyards: *open-air spaces enclosed by buildings*

crawl: *a way of swimming, by moving first one arm and then the other over your head while kicking your legs*

disadvantage: *something that makes it harder to succeed*

disaster: *a terrible event*

ecomuseum: *a museum where you can learn about certain animals and where they live*

ecosystem: *all of the plants and animals that live in a particular area and have an effect on one another*

feast: *a large meal, often part of a party or celebration*

fishy: *causing a feeling that something is wrong*

fragrant: *pleasant-smelling*

frustrating: *upsetting; irritating*

"gave me his/her word": *made a promise*

glumly: *sadly*

habitats: *places where plants or animals usually live*

high tide: *the time of day when the water in an ocean is at its highest (tides are the daily rise and fall of sea level)*

home base: *the last base in a game, such as baseball, that the players aim to reach*

horsing around: *being silly, especially in a physical way*

impression: *pressing a hard object into something soft, such as clay, in order to copy its shape*

jiffy: *in no time*

lyrics: *the words to a song*

marine biologist: *a scientist who studies ocean life*

moat: *a deep ditch, filled with water, surrounding a castle*

"out of the blue": *suddenly, for no apparent reason*

pen pals: *two people, often living far away from each other, who stay friends by writing letters*

piggyback fight: *a game, usually played in the water, where half of the players climb on the other players' shoulders, and then try to knock other players down*

plankton: *tiny creatures that float in the ocean*

plaster of Paris: *a powder that becomes a quick-drying plaster when mixed with water*

replicas: *perfect copies of an original object*

rest stop: *a place to pull off the road and take a break, usually by the side of a highway*

salt marsh: *land near the ocean that sometimes floods with salt water*

scaredy-cat: *a timid or frightened person*

scuba diving instructor: *someone who teaches you how to use underwater diving equipment*

shipshape: *neat and tidy*

shrugged: *raising and lowering shoulders as if to say "I don't know"*

sifted: *carefully sorted*

sing-along: *a group of people singing together, usually in a casual way*

s'mores: *a dessert made of graham crackers, marshmallows and chocolate*

spouting: *a whale blowing out air when it comes to the surface of the ocean, which often looks like a fountain of water*

stick-in-the-mud: *someone who dislikes trying new things*

symbol: *an object that stands for something else*

tagged: *fitted with a "tag," a tiny, harmless device that is attached to an animal in order to track its movements*

these are **my** favorite shells:

The Power of a Girl

For every *Our Generation*® product you buy, a portion of sales goes to Free The Children's Power of a Girl Initiative to help provide girls in developing countries an education—the most powerful tool in the world for escaping poverty.

Did you know that out of the millions of children who aren't in school, 70% of them are girls? In developing communities around the world, many girls can't go to school. Usually it's because there's no school available or because their responsibilities to family (farming, earning an income, walking hours each day for water) prevent it.

Over the past two years, Free The Children has had incredible success with its Year of Water and Year of Education initiatives, providing 100,000 people with clean water for life and building 200 classrooms for overseas communities. This year, they celebrate the Year of Empowerment, focusing on supporting alternative income projects for sustainable development.

The most incredible part is that most of Free The Children's funding comes from kids just like you, holding lemonade stands, bake sales, penny drives, walkathons and more.

Just by buying an *Our Generation* product you have helped change the world, and you are powerful (beyond belief!) to help even more.

If you want to find out more, visit:
www.ogdolls.com/free-the-children

FREE THE CHILDREN
children helping children through education

Free The Children provided the factual information pertaining to their organization. Free The Children is a 501c3 organization.

this is **our** story

We are an extraordinary generation of girls. And have we got a story to tell.

Our Generation® is unlike any that has come before. We're helping our families learn to recycle, holding bake sales to support charities, and holding penny drives to build homes for orphaned children in Haiti. We're helping our little sisters learn to read and even making sure the new kid at school has a place to sit in the cafeteria.

All that and we still find time to play hopscotch and hockey. To climb trees, do cartwheels all the way down the block and laugh with our friends until milk comes out of our noses. You know, to be kids.

Will we have a big impact on the world? We already have. What's ahead for us? What's ahead for the world? We have no idea. We're too busy grabbing and holding on to the joy that is today.

Yep. This is our time. This is our story.

www.ogdolls.com

About the Author

Erika Nadine White lives with her family in a small village by a lake. She has been writing poetry and fiction for most of her life. This is her second story for children.

About the Illustrator

Passionate about drawing from an early age, Géraldine decided to pursue her studies in computer multimedia in order to further develop her style and technique. Her favorite themes to explore in her illustrations are fashion and urban life. In her free time, Géraldine loves to paint and travel. She is passionate about horses and loves spending time at the stable. It's where she feels most at peace and gives her time to think and fuel her creativity.

This story came to life because of all the wonderful people who contributed their creativity and vision, including Joe Battat, Dany Battat, Loredana Ramacieri, Véronique Casavant, Véronique Chartrand, Sandy Jacinto, Jenny Gambino, Natalie Cohen, Ralph de Smit, Kirsten Shute, Veronica Sorcher, Karen Woods and Donna Yakibchuk.